THE CHILDREN'S CLASSICS Collection

Volume 2

Dados Internacionais de Catalogação na Publicação (CIP) de acordo com ISBD

S487t Stevenson, Robert Louis.
Treasure Island / Robert Louis Stevenson. - Jandira, SP : W. Books, 2025.
120 p. : 12,80cm x 19,80cm. - (Classics).

ISBN: 978-65-5294-208-1

1. Literatura inglesa. 2. Séries. 3. Clássicos. 4. Filmes. 5. Aventura. I. Título. II. Série.

2025-2502 CDD 820
CDU 821.111-3

Elaborada por Lucio Feitosa - CRB-8/8803
Índice para catálogo sistemático:
1. Literatura inglesa 820
2. Literatura inglesa 821.111-3

Text based on the original story by Robert Louis Stevenson,
adapted by Catherine Veitch
Illustrations by Archina Laezza

1st edition in 2025
www.cirandacultural.com.br

Treasure Island

Robert Louis Stevenson

W. Books

Jim Hawkins

The narrator

Doctor Livesey

A doctor and magistrate

Squire Trelawney

A nobleman

Captain Smollett

An experienced sailor

Long John Silver

Lost his leg on
one voyage

Captain Flint

Long John
Silver's parrot

Billy Bones

Also known as
the Captain

Pew

Lost his sight on
one voyage

Israel Hands

Steers the ship

Ben Gunn

Marooned on
Treasure Island

Chapter One

My name is Jim Hawkins. I'll begin my tale about Treasure Island from when I first met Billy Bones. I didn't know that was his name then, so I simply called him the Captain. My tale is one of adventure, bravery, trickery, mutiny, mystery and treasure!

mutiny
Openly disobeying or fighting against the leaders in charge.

I remember, like it was yesterday, the day that the Captain arrived at my father's inn, the Admiral Benbow. He was a tall, strong man, with his hair in a tar-stained plait falling over one shoulder of his dirty blue coat. His hands were rough and scarred, with black, broken nails, and he had a scar across one cheek.

When he arrived at the Admiral Benbow, he had a large sailor's sea-chest and was whistling an old sea shanty (this was a song I would hear many more times). It went:

'Fifteen men on the dead man's chest, yo-ho-ho, and off we go!'

The Captain took a room at our inn. He was a quiet, stern man, who liked to be left alone. He spent

his days outside, looking through a brass telescope. Then in the evenings he sat in a corner of the inn next to the fire, drinking strong black tea. People who came into the inn learnt not to bother him.

Every day when the Captain came back inside after looking through his telescope, he would ask whether any sailors had visited. At first we thought he was looking for the company of sailors like himself, but we soon realised that he wanted to avoid them. The Captain asked me to keep my eyes open for a sailor with one leg, and to let him know the moment he appeared.

The Captain stayed on at our inn for many months, long after his money had run out. But my poor father was not brave enough to ask him for any more.

One frosty January morning, after a visit from a stranger, we learnt the Captain's real name.

The Captain had gone for a stroll and I was laying the breakfast table, when a man entered the inn. He was pale, with two fingers missing from his left hand, and he carried a cutlass like the Captain.

'Are you setting this table for my mate, Billy Bones?' the stranger asked. He gave me an unpleasant look.

I told him I did not know anyone

cutlass
A short, thick sword with one cutting edge and a curved blade.

called Billy. This table was for the Captain, who was staying at our inn.

'Well,' said the stranger. 'My mate Bill likes to be called the Captain. He has a scar across one cheek and a stern manner about him.'

It was clear that the Captain and Bill must be the same person.

Chapter Two

The stranger waited inside with me, and soon the Captain returned. He marched across the room to his breakfast on the table, without looking to the right or left.

'Bill,' said the stranger in a loud, booming voice.

The Captain turned round. All the colour drained from his face, and he looked like he had seen a ghost.

'Remember me, Bill, your old

shipmate?' asked the stranger.

'Black Dog!' gasped the Captain. 'What do you want?'

Black Dog asked for a cup of strong black tea, and then he and the Captain sat down and talked in low whispers. I could not hear what they were saying at first. But as their voices grew louder, I managed to pick up a word or two.

'No, no, no! That's an end to it!' cried the Captain. And then, 'If it comes to a fight, then let's fight!'

All of a sudden, there was a tremendous noise as the two men shouted at each other. A chair and table were sent flying, and the men's swords clashed as they fought. Black Dog cried out in pain as the Captain's sword struck his shoulder and drew blood. Their fight spilled out onto the street. Realising he was no match for the Captain, Black Dog turned and ran off.

The Captain looked exhausted and could barely stand. I ran to fetch him some tea, but heard a loud crash and ran back to find the Captain lying on the floor. At the same time, my mother, who had heard all the noise, came running downstairs. Between us, we raised the Captain's head. He was breathing very loud and hard, but his eyes were closed and his face was a horrible colour.

Luckily, Doctor Livesey was visiting my sick father upstairs at

the time. The doctor was also a magistrate and was used to dealing with trouble. The good doctor examined the Captain.

Between us, we managed to carry the Captain upstairs and laid him on his bed.

'This man has had a stroke,' the doctor said. He told us that the Captain needed to rest.

A few days later, I brought some cool drinks and medicines up to the Captain in his room.

magistrate

A judge of a local court that deals with less serious crimes.

'Jim', the Captain said, and beckoned me closer. 'That Black Dog is a rotten man. All of old Flint's crew are.'

'Who is Flint?' I asked.

'He was the most terrifying pirate captain that did ever set sail!' he replied. 'Now his crew have found me and they are after my old sea chest.'

The Captain pointed to the old chest he had brought with him, which he never let anyone near. He continued his story.

'I sailed with Flint and he gave me that sea chest as he lay dying. You must fetch that Doctor Livesey and tell him to bring as many people as he can to the inn. Hurry, before I'm given the black spot.'

'What is the black spot, Captain?' I asked.

'It's a pirate death threat!' he replied.

The Captain rambled on a little longer, his voice growing weaker. As soon as the medicine took effect, he fell into a heavy sleep and I left his room.

Chapter Three

I should have rushed off to fetch Doctor Livesey, but other events distracted me. My poor father left this world. I was so busy organising his funeral, letting people know and running the inn with my mother, that I forgot all about the Captain's troubles.

The day after my father's funeral, events took another turn. The Captain was a little stronger and well enough to sit in a quiet corner downstairs. On this day, a second stranger came by the inn. He was blind, and tapped the ground in front of him with a stick. He looked old and frail, huddled in an oversized, tatty cloak with a hood, and he wore a green shade over his eyes.

'Will you give me your hand, my kind, young friend?' he asked.

I held out my hand and the stranger gripped it tightly. I was startled and tried to pull away, but the blind man was strong and tugged me closer to him.

'Now, boy,' he said, 'take me straight to the Captain, or I'll break your arm.'

He wrenched my arm as he spoke and made me cry out. I had never heard a voice so cruel and cold. I obeyed him at once and led him to where the sick old Captain was sitting. The poor Captain raised his eyes and looked in terror at the stranger. He tried to get up, but did not have enough strength left in his body.

'Hold out your hand, Bill,' the stranger said to the Captain.

I saw the stranger press something into the Captain's hand, which closed upon it instantly.

'And now that's done,' said the stranger. As he left the inn, I could hear his stick tap-tap-tapping into the distance.

The Captain opened his hand. He was holding a piece of paper marked with a large black spot.

'I don't have long to live!' the Captain cried, and he lurched to his feet.

As he did, he swayed, put his hand to his throat and then, with a peculiar sound, fell face-down onto the floor.

I ran to him at once, calling out to my mother. But the Captain was dead. I couldn't help but burst into tears. It was the second death in a short time, and the sorrow of losing my father was still fresh in my heart.

Chapter Four

I told my mother everything that the Captain had told me about the sailors and his sea chest.

'I will not lose money that is due to you, my fatherless boy,' Mother said. 'We will open the Captain's sea chest and take what is owed to us.'

We had to search the Captain for a key to his sea chest. I knelt down and felt in his pockets, one after the other. I found a few small coins, some tobacco, a small knife and a pocket compass.

'Perhaps it's around his neck?' suggested my mother.

Feeling rather sick, I tore open the Captain's shirt at the neck. Hanging on a grimy bit of string was a key. I used the small knife to cut the string, then we excitedly hurried upstairs to the little room where he had stayed. It was where his sea chest had stood since the day of his arrival.

The chest's lock was stiff, but my mother forced the key and threw back the lid with surprising strength. The inside smelt strongly of tobacco and tar. All we could see on the top were some fine clothes, carefully brushed and folded. Under those were all kinds of things: a tin cup, tobacco, two pistols, a bar of silver, an old Spanish watch, some strange shells, a pair of compasses and some other little trinkets of no value. Underneath these things was an old coat, whitened from sea salt. My mother pulled it out hastily. The last thing in the chest

trinket

A small decorative object, or a piece of jewellery that is cheap or of low quality.

was a bundle tied up in an oily cloth. It contained papers and a pile of coins.

'I'm an honest woman,' said my mother. 'I'll take what is owed to us, and not a penny more.'

As she counted out some coins into her bag, I heard the tapping of a stick on the pavement outside.

It could only be the blind stranger returning. We sat still, holding our breath. There was a sharp rap on the inn door, and then the door rattled as the rogue tried to enter. Thankfully, it was locked. The tapping started up again, as the blind man walked away.

'Mother,' I said quietly, 'there is no time to count out the coins. Just take them all. We must leave here now.'

I knew the blind man would return, and that he would most likely bring others, too.

Just then, we heard a little low whistle from up the hill. Someone else was coming.

'I'll take what coins I have,' said my mother, jumping to her feet.

'And I'll take this to make up what we are owed,' I said, picking up the papers wrapped in the oily cloth.

We scrambled downstairs in the dark, not daring to use a candle. Then we hurried out into the cold, black night. We hid under a bridge just in time to hear the sound of several people's footsteps running towards the inn.

Chapter Five

My curiosity got the better of me. Despite my fear, I peered out to

see what was going on. In the moonlight, I saw several men standing outside the inn. With them was the blind man, who I learnt was called Pew.

'Down with the door!' cried the blind man.

'Aye, aye, sir!' answered the men. Three men rushed at the

inn door but were surprised to find it open, and they fell through the doorway. I heard a voice from inside shout, 'Bill's dead!'

'Search him, you lazy lot! And the rest of you, go upstairs and open the chest!' cried the blind man.

From our hiding place, I heard feet running heavily up the old stairs. Shortly after, the window of the Captain's room was flung open with such force that it shattered the glass. A man leant out.

'Is it there?' roared the blind man.

'Someone's got here before us, Pew,' replied the man. 'There's only some money left.'

'It's that boy from the inn – I wish I had put his eyes out!' cursed Pew. 'Find him!' he shouted to his men, striking his stick on the road. The men tore through the inn looking for me. I could hear them knocking over furniture and kicking down doors.

They were interrupted by the sound of horses galloping over the hill. People from the neighbouring village had seen the men approaching our inn and had come to help. The sailors at once ran off in different directions, leaving Pew behind. The blind man took a wrong turn and stumbled a few steps towards the approaching horses.

'Johnny! Black Dog! Dirk!' he called out. 'You wouldn't leave your old mate, Pew?'

In the moonlight, I saw four or five riders gallop at full speed. Pew heard them, too, and realised his mistake. He tried to scramble out of the way, but instead ran straight into them. Unable to stop, the horses trampled over him and he fell on his side, stone dead.

The riders were horrified. After much debate, they took my mother back to their village while I returned to the Admiral Benbow with Mr Dance, one of the horsemen. The inn had been

wrecked by the unruly sailors. Surprisingly, the only thing they had taken was some silver from the till. I guessed that they were not after the Captain's money, but the papers I had taken. Mr Dance offered to take the papers from me, but I wanted to give them to Doctor Livesey, who was the magistrate.

'Quite right,' replied Mr Dance. 'I'll take you there.'

So we set off to find Doctor Livesey.

Chapter Six

We found Doctor Livesey dining with Squire Trelawney. A servant showed us into a great library lined with bookcases, where the squire and the doctor sat beside an open fire. Mr Dance told our story. The doctor asked me for the papers, and I gave him the oily package. He looked it over as if his fingers were itching to open it,

squire
In the past, a man who owned most of the land around a village in England.

then tucked it in his coat pocket. Mr Dance was thanked for his help and then told he could go home. At the doctor's suggestion I was given some tasty pigeon pie.

While I tucked into the delicious food, Doctor Livesey and Squire Trelawney discussed what had happened.

'Have you heard of this Flint?' the doctor asked.

'Of course I have! He was the blood-thirstiest pirate that ever sailed the seas,' replied Trelawney.

‘Well, if Jim agrees, we’ll open the packet,’ said the doctor, looking at me. I nodded, eagerly. He laid it before him on the table. The oily bundle was sewn together, and the doctor had to get out his instrument case and cut the stitches with his medical scissors.

A map of an island fell out. Marked on it were coordinates,

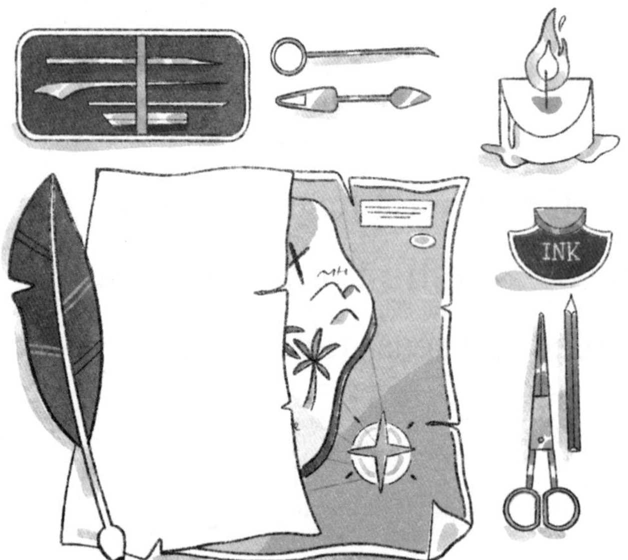

the names of hills and bays, and three tall trees. There were some extra crosses of red ink: two on the north of the island and one in the south. Beside the cross in the south, in small, neat handwriting in the same red ink, was written: ‘Bulk of treasure here.’

coordinates

Numbers and/or letters that show the exact position of a point on a map.

All of this information was a muddle to me, but it made the doctor and the squire very excited.

'Livesey,' cried the squire. 'You must leave your doctoring duties at once. We will find a ship and the best crew in England, and sail to this Treasure Island. Jim will be a cabin-boy. You, Livesey, will be the ship's doctor, and I will be the admiral.'

We all agreed on his daring plan.

The squire had no trouble finding a ship and a crew, and after

admiral
Someone who leads and controls a ship or military group.

spreading the word we were sailing for treasure! He found a man called Long John Silver, who had lost a leg but had been at sea for many years. Silver got together a bunch of tough old sailors, and he volunteered to be the ship's cook.

Hearing that the squire had told people about the treasure made me uneasy. I feared the one-legged man may have been the same man Billy Bones had spoken of. But I did my best to put those thoughts out of my mind, and looked forward to an adventure at sea.

Chapter Seven

Squire Trelawney, Doctor Livesey and I were saluted as we boarded our ship, called the *Hispaniola*. However, it appeared that the captain, Captain Smollett, was angry

with everyone and everything on board.

'Are we almost ready to sail?' the squire asked.

'Well, sir, allow me to speak my mind,' said the captain. 'I don't like this voyage, and I don't like the crew.'

The squire looked angry at this, but Doctor Livesey quickly stepped forward.

'Now, Captain Smollett, what is wrong?' he asked.

'I don't like treasure voyages at all, and especially when they are kept a secret,' Smollett said. 'I've heard that you have a map of an island, and there are crosses on the map to show where the treasure is.'

'I never told anyone that,' said the squire fiercely.

'Well, all the sailors knew before they came on board, sir,' replied the captain. 'But I will sail your ship, so long as you keep where the map is hidden a secret.'

And with that, Smollett went back to his duties.

All night we rushed about to make sure that we had all the supplies we needed on board. Just before dawn, the boatswain blew his pipe and the crew raised the anchor. Despite being tired, I stayed on deck to watch everything. It was all so new and exciting to me – the commands, the shrill sound

boatswain

Someone who is in charge of a ship's equipment and crew.

of the whistle, the men bustling to their places by the soft glimmer of the ship's lanterns.

'Barbecue, start us a song,' cried a voice. Barbecue was what the crew called Long John Silver.

'Aye, aye, mates,' said Silver, who was standing by, with his crutch under his arm. He at once broke out into a song, and I knew the words as well:

'Fifteen men on the dead man's chest ...'

And then the whole crew sang the chorus:

'... yo-ho-ho, and off we go!'

The sails of the great ship billowed in the wind, and at last, the *Hispaniola* began her voyage to Treasure Island.

Chapter Eight

I will not go into every detail of our voyage, but there are two things that I need to tell you about.

First, there was Long John Silver, our ship's cook. All the crew respected and obeyed him. He had a way of talking to each person and making them feel special. He was always very kind to me, and happy to see me in his kitchen. He had

a pet parrot, which he jokingly called Captain Flint, and he kept her in a cage in one corner. The parrot had the habit of squawking 'Pieces of eight! Pieces of eight! Pieces of eight!', which I learnt were Spanish coins.

Second, there was the barrel of apples. We had some harsh weather on the voyage and many of the sailors were seasick, but the squire helped to raise spirits by placing a barrel of apples on deck.

When a man had worked hard, he helped himself to an apple.

'It's not good to spoil the crew like that,' Captain Smollett moaned to Doctor Livesey.

But something good *did* come from it. Had it not been for the barrel, we would never have had the warning, and possibly might all have been killed ...

This was how it happened.

It was the last night of our voyage, and we were expecting to see Treasure Island some time

before the next morning. We had a steady breeze and a quiet sea. The *Hispaniola* gently bobbed over the water. Everyone was excited because we were so near to the end of the first part of our adventure.

When all my work was done for the day, I thought I would help myself to an apple. The night watch was on careful lookout for the island. One of the men was steering the ship and whistling softly to himself. It was the only other sound apart from the rhythmic swish of the sea against the ship. There weren't many apples left, so I climbed into the barrel to feel around. As I was squatted in the dark, a large man sat down nearby. I was about to jump out when the man began to speak. It was Silver, and on hearing what he said, I knew I had to stay hidden. The lives of all the honest men on that ship depended on me listening to every word.

Chapter Nine

'Flint was captain and I worked as the ship's cook,' boasted Silver. 'I lost my leg on that voyage. The same voyage that my mate Pew lost his sight.'

'Ah!' cried a young voice, who I guessed was Israel Hands. He was one of the crew who steered the ship. 'Flint was the best of them all!'

'I have nearly 3,000 pounds safely hidden in the bank from my voyages. Where are Flint's crew, I hear you ask? Why, most of them are here, in disguise, on board the *Hispaniola*!'

You may imagine how I felt when I heard Silver boasting about the wicked men he had worked with in the past, men he had pretended he did not know, and that some of them were on this ship. If I had been able, I would have killed him through the barrel.

The conversation was about to take an even worse turn. Silver gave a little whistle, and a third man joined them.

'What I want to know, Barbecue, is how long are we going to stay with these wretched people? I'm fed up with old Smollett,' said Israel Hands impatiently.

'Listen up,' said Silver. 'We need Captain Smollett to sail this ship for us. And I don't know where the map is, so we need the squire and the doctor to find the treasure for us. We will get rid of them when the time is right. Now jump up and fetch me an apple from the barrel.'

You can imagine the terror I felt on hearing those words! I would have leapt out and run for it if I felt strong enough, but my limbs and heart felt weak. I heard the young Israel get up, but then, thankfully, one of the others stopped him.

'Forget that! Let's have a strong black tea, instead.'

As the trio drank their tea, Silver made a toast:

'Here's to old Flint and his treasure,' he said.

At that moment, the lookout shouted, 'Land ahoy!'

We had arrived at Treasure Island.

There was the sound of feet rushing across the deck as the sailors left their cabins below and came up topside to see the island. It was easy for me to slip out of the apple barrel and below deck unseen.

I found the doctor, the squire and the captain studying a map of Treasure Island. I told them the details of Silver's conversation that I had overheard.

'We must go on. If I gave the word to turn around, they would mutiny at once,' said Smollett. We agreed that we had to carry on as if everything was fine. But we would have to keep our eyes and ears open.

Chapter Ten

It was sweltering hot and many of the crew were restless, so it was agreed that they could stretch their legs ashore. An idea popped into my head that would later help to save our lives. I was not needed on the ship, so I thought I would sneak ashore along with the crew. I quickly slipped under a seat in one of the rowing boats and hid.

As the boat was rowed to the

shore, we passed under some overhanging trees. I quickly reached up, grabbed a branch, swung out of the boat unseen and plunged into the thick bushes. It was exciting to explore a new, strange land. I crossed a marshland full of willows and bulrushes. There were flowers that

I did not know the names of, and a few snakes. After a while, I heard some voices and guessed that my shipmates must be close by.

I crawled under the nearest bush and peeped out, making sure to stay as quiet as a mouse. As the voices came nearer, I heard Silver speak to one of the crew called Tom. Silver was trying to persuade Tom to join his gang. But Tom was an honest man and refused, saying he would not turn against his captain or his duty.

And with that, brave Tom turned his back on Silver and

walked away. But he did not get far. Silver seized the branch of a tree and threw it like a missile through the air.

It struck poor Tom in the middle of his back. Tom's hands flew up, then he gave a sort of gasp and fell down dead.

As if nothing terrible had happened, Silver put his hand into his pocket and brought out a whistle. He blew it several times. I felt scared. More men would be coming, and I might be discovered. They had killed Tom. Would I be next? I could not go back to the ship. Even if I made it back, after what I had seen, I could not pretend that everything was fine. Silver would guess that I knew he was a murderer. It was all over. I breathed a quiet goodbye to the *Hispaniola*, the squire, the doctor and the captain, and I ran.

Chapter Eleven

I reached a steep, stony hill. Just ahead, a creature jumped out from behind a pine tree. The creature was dark and scruffy, and I did not know if it was a bear, a monkey or a man.

'Who or what are you?' I gasped.

'Ben Gunn,' the creature replied. I could now see that he was a man. His voice sounded hoarse and awkward, like a rusty lock. 'I haven't spoken to anyone for the last three years.'

His skin had been burnt by years in the hot sun and his lips were cracked. He was dressed in ragged pieces of cloth that must have been a ship's sail once.

'Were you shipwrecked?' I asked.

'No, mate,' he replied. 'I was marooned.'

I had heard the word before and knew it was a horrible kind of punishment, one where a person was left alone on some empty, distant island.

marooned
Left in a place from which you cannot escape.

'I have survived by eating goats, oysters and berries. Do you have any cheese on you? I've dreamt of eating cheese for many nights!'

'If we ever get back home,' I said, 'you can eat all the cheese you want.'

I introduced myself to Ben, and told him the story of our voyage and the trouble that we were now in. He listened carefully before looking around, then lowered his voice.

'I'm rich,' he said.

I was sure that the poor fellow had gone crazy, living on his own for so long. Seeing I did not believe him, he repeated it.

'Rich! Rich! And I'll help you, Jim, if you will help me to escape from this island!'

Ben told me he knew Flint's crew, including Billy Bones and Long John Silver. He said that Flint had hidden his treasure on this island.

'I can help you find it, if you let me sail home with you,' he said. 'I have a boat I made that's hidden under a large rock. It won't carry

us across the ocean, but we could row it back to your boat.'

Just then, we heard the thunder of cannon fire ring out across the island.

'They have started fighting!' I cried, realising that the pirates must have finally revealed themselves and attacked the rest of the *Hispaniola*'s - roman crew.

'Follow me,' said Ben.

As we followed the sounds of fighting, Ben led me to a hut where my friends were sheltering from the pirates' attack. When he saw the crew, he did not want to meet my captain or the doctor or squire, which I thought must be because of his past. He left me to go inside. I was so happy to be reunited with my friends again. I told them about my time on the island, and about Ben Gunn. Doctor Livesey told me how they had followed me to the island as they feared for my safety amongst the rough pirates. He then told me what had happened since they landed on the island.

Chapter Twelve

The doctor described how Silver and the other pirates who ventured onto the island had quickly found them in the hut, and a fight had broken out between the two groups. The pirates who had remained on the *Hispaniola* fired cannonballs at the hut from the ship, but luckily they all missed.

My friends may have won the small battle and defended the hut, but I could clearly see the price they had paid for that victory. Many of my crewmates were injured and some lay on the ground, stunned, while others would never leave this island again. The squire had his arm around the captain, supporting him and keeping him upright. He looked very pale.

The pirates did not return that day. This gave the doctor some time to treat the wounded on both sides, and for the squire and I to cook dinner. The captain's wounds were serious, but not life-threatening.

He had broken his shoulder and torn some muscles in his calf. The doctor said he would recover eventually, but he must try not to walk or move his arm.

After dinner, the doctor put the treasure map in his pocket and a musket over his shoulder and hurried off through the trees. I guessed he was going to find Ben Gunn. I was right, as I learnt later on.

I envied the doctor walking through the cool woods, when

musket
A type of gun used in the past.

I was so hot inside the hut that my clothes were sticking to me. A thought steadily grew in my head. *What if the Hispaniola was set adrift? The pirates would not be able to escape the island or fire the cannons at us*. Rather recklessly, I decided to leave the safety of my crewmates and the hut, and see if it was possible to carry out my idea. When no one was looking, I filled my pockets with biscuits, grabbed two pistols and sneaked out of the hut.

I was going to find the large rock where Ben Gunn had hidden his boat. It was getting dark and fog was coming in. I could see a large rock in the distance, but it was a long way off. I crawled through scrub, often on all fours, and eventually reached the rock. I found a little goatskin tent hidden in some bushes near the rock.

I lifted one side of the tent, and in the moonlight saw Ben Gunn's little round boat. It looked home-made, with goatskin stretched over a wooden frame. It was very small, even for me. I did not know at the time, but the boat was a coracle. The one good thing about it was that it was light and easy to carry.

Now that I had found the boat, you would have thought this would be the end of my silly ideas. But another one popped into my

coracle
A small, round boat made by stretching animal skin over a wooden frame.

head – now that a fog had rolled in, it was the perfect opportunity to slip out under the cover of darkness and cut the *Hispaniola* from her anchor.

I had a meal of some biscuits, then carried the coracle over my shoulder and stumbled down to shore. A little way off, I could see some of the pirates sleeping around a huge fire. The *Hispaniola* was a way out to sea. I quietly set the coracle on the water.

Steering the circular boat was not easy, as it kept leaning over to one side. If it wasn't for the tide pushing me out, I don't think I would have made it to the *Hispaniola*. But at last, I reached the ship and carefully cut through the thick anchor rope with my knife. Once it was free, the *Hispaniola* drifted along on the rising swell of waves and towards the shallow waters of the beach.

To my horror, my little boat was directly between the shore and the ship. If I did not do something quickly, the coracle would be smashed and sunk by the larger ship.

Chapter Thirteen

I heard shouts and the pounding of feet on board the *Hispaniola*, as the pirates realised that something was wrong. I was sure this was the end for me. Either my boat would be smashed to pieces or the pirates would spot me.

I knew I had no choice but to climb aboard the *Hispaniola*. I stood up in the coracle, grabbed part of the ship and flung myself onto the deck. I glanced back to see my coracle smashed to bits against the ship. Now I had no way of returning to the shore until the *Hispaniola* ran aground.

I moved slowly and cautiously, not wanting to be caught by the pirates on board, but after a few moments, I still could not see anyone on deck. However, after some searching, I came across two members of the crew. One was lying on his back, stone dead. And Israel Hands was badly injured.

'Where might you have come from?' he asked, his injuries too severe for him to move.

'I've come aboard to take control of this ship, Mr Hands. So you can call me Captain Hawkins from now on,' I replied.

Hands looked at me thoughtfully. 'I suppose, *Captain* Hawkins, you will want to get back to the island.'

We made a deal. Hands would help me sail the *Hispaniola* back to shore, and I would give him food, drink and medical help. I did not trust Hands but there was no other option.

I bandaged Hands's bleeding wound with a silk handkerchief of my mother's that I had brought with me, and Hands guided me as I sailed the ship north of the island and into a bay. As I turned around to speak, Hands rushed towards me with a knife.

The *Hispaniola* drifted into shallow water and struck the sandy seabed. The jolt sent us both flying across the deck and we fell into a scuffle. I kicked myself free of his grasp and escaped by climbing up the tilting mast. Hands hauled himself up the

mast after me, with his knife in his teeth, dragging his wounded leg behind him. I reached for my two pistols and shouted at him to stay where he was.

I was about to order him to climb back down, when something sharp flew through the air. Hands had thrown his knife at me. It grazed my shoulder and I fell against the mast, accidentally squeezing the triggers on my pistols, which I then dropped in surprise. Hands cried out and fell head first into the water. Sick, faint and terrified, I watched as he sank for good.

I was now alone on the ship. I had to find my friends on Treasure Island. Fortunately, the *Hispaniola* had drifted close enough to the land for me to swim safely to shore. I left the ship that was now beached and leaning to one side, and set off to find my friends.

Chapter Fourteen

Using the light of the moon to guide me, I found my way over the island and back to the hut where I had left my friends. From inside the hut, I could hear their snores, but it was so dark I could not see anyone. Something did not seem quite right. I paused before carefully entering the hut.

Suddenly, a shrill voice cried out in the darkness. 'Pieces of eight! Pieces of eight! Pieces of eight!'

It repeated it over and over again.

It was Silver's parrot, Captain Flint! She was a better watch than any of the men and had alerted them to my arrival. I had no time to escape. The sleeping men sprang up immediately, and one of them grabbed me.

The pirates were in control of the hut and all the supplies. I could not see my friends and was afraid they had all been killed.

'Shiver my timbers,' said Silver.

'It's nice of you to drop in on us, Hawkins.'

I did not answer.

'You remind me of myself when I was young,' he continued. 'The doctor is very angry that you ran away. They are glad to be rid of you, so it looks like you will have to join my crew.'

It was good to hear that my friends were still alive. My friends may be angry but I didn't believe that they were glad to be rid of me.

There was no way I was going to join Silver and his men.

Lifting my chin, I proudly told

him everything I had done: from overhearing his plans when I was crouched in the apple barrel, to cutting the *Hispaniola*'s - roman anchor rope and taking back control of the ship.

'I don't fear you any more than I fear a fly,' I said. 'But if you spare me, I'll speak up for you when you are in court.'

One of the pirates sprang at me with his arms raised. But Silver lifted his hand to hold him back. '*I* am the captain here!' he said coldly, before moving closer to me. 'We could each help other,' he whispered in my ear. ‘If you agree to speak for me when we return to England, and save me from being hanged for my crimes, then I will make sure you get out of this situation unharmed.’

I reluctantly agreed. Still whispering in my ear, he said, ‘My men have been promised treasure, and so far they have had none.

You will need to pretend to be my hostage, otherwise the men will never trust me and you will never leave this island.' Turning towards his men, he shouted, 'We have a prisoner and a treasure hunt ahead of us!'

With a dramatic gesture, Silver threw down the treasure map, and the pirates leapt on it like cats on a mouse. They passed it from hand to hand, each one tearing it away from the last.

Silver looked at me and grinned. 'Your beloved doctor gave it to me.'

'Who is going to lead you to the treasure?' he roared at his men.

'Silver!' they all cried. 'Barbecue for captain!'

I went to sleep that night feeling a little safer with the men back on Silver's side. However, I did not fully trust Silver, and could not understand why the doctor had given him the map.

Chapter Fifteen

The next morning, we set off to search for the treasure. We were a strange group. The parrot, Captain Flint, was perched on Silver's shoulder and chatting nonsense non-stop. Silver was holding a rope that was tied around my waist, and all the men were carrying weapons, except for me. Some men also carried axes and spades.

We had been walking through the thick undergrowth for a while, pausing every now and then to look at the map, when Silver spotted two tall trees that rose above the bushes.

'Look there! Those are the trees from the map. This is so easy that a child could find the treasure,' he said.

'I'm not sure,' growled Morgan. 'Think about how crafty Flint is.'

'Well, be thankful that he's no longer around,' said Silver.

Suddenly, a trembling voice sang out these well-known words from the amongst the trees:

'Fifteen men on the dead man's chest, yo-ho-ho, and off we go!'

I have never seen men more shocked than this group of pirates. The colour drained from their faces. Some leapt into the air, while others grabbed hold of each other.

One pirate slumped to the ground and whimpered, ‘It’s the ghost of Flint!’

‘Come now, lads,’ said Silver, struggling to get his words out. ‘It’s someone messing about.’

‘Fetch me some tea, Darby!’ wailed the voice.

The pirates stood still, their eyes popping out of their heads.

‘They were Flint’s last words,’ moaned another pirate called Morgan.

I could hear Silver’s teeth rattle in his head, but he was still not ready to give up.

‘Shipmates,’ he cried, ‘I’m here to get the treasure, and I’ll not be stopped by man or ghost.’

The pirates were too terrified to reply, but they were also too scared to run, and kept very close to Silver as we slowly walked on.

It was not long before we reached the first of the tall trees, and then the second. The tree rose nearly 200 feet above us. But it was not its size that impressed the pirates, it was knowing that 700,000 pounds in gold lay buried somewhere beneath its huge shadow.

Silver hobbled forwards on his crutch, tugging roughly at the rope that held me, urging me to hurry. Every now and then he turned back and gave me a curious look. With gold so near, I was sure he had forgotten his promise and that he hoped to grab the treasure, find and board the *Hispaniola* under the cover of night, and sail away as a rich man.

Chapter Sixteen

Suddenly, a low cry rang out and the pirates stopped walking, but Silver quickened his pace, stamping his crutch on the ground like he was possessed. In front of us was a huge hole. It had obviously been dug a long while ago, as the sides had fallen in and grass was growing at the bottom. There was also a broken pickaxe on the ground. It was clear that the treasure had already been discovered.

The 700,000 pounds were gone!

The pirates leapt into the hole and started digging with their fingers, searching for any treasure left.

Silver knew he was beaten.

He guessed the pirates would be angry.

Silver backed away slowly, pulling me with him. 'Jim,' he whispered, 'take this and get ready for trouble.'

He passed me a pistol.

Morgan held up a piece of gold from the bottom of the hole. It was a two-guinea piece.

'Two guineas!' roared Morgan, shaking it at Silver. 'That's your 700,000 pounds, is it?'

The pirates scrambled angrily

guinea

An old British gold coin worth £1.05.

out of the hole, on the opposite side to Silver and I.

'Mates,' cried one of the pirates, 'there are only two of them! The one who got us all into this mess in the first place and that young lad who has been ruining our plans. Let's finish them off and see to it they never leave this island!'

Suddenly, there was a loud, *Crack! Crack! Crack!* Three shots rang out from the trees.

Two pirates tumbled head first into the hole, while the others turned and ran into the forest.

The doctor, Ben Gunn and another of our crew, Abraham Gray, strode into sight.

'Quick, lads,' the doctor said. 'We must stop them before they reach the small boats. We can't have them escaping the island!'

Silver quickly untied the rope that bound me and we all gave chase. We set off at a fast pace, plunging through brambles up to our chests. Thankfully, the fleeing pirates did not seem to have any kind of plan and we reached the small boats first.

The doctor destroyed one of the boats with a pickaxe, so that when the escaped pirates realised we were not chasing them anymore they could not use it. Then we boarded the other boat and sailed around the island to Ben Gunn's cave.

Ben's cave was large and overhung with ferns. It had a sandy floor and there was a little spring which bubbled water into a cool, clear pool. Inside, lying beside a big fire was Captain Smollett. I was overjoyed to see

that he had survived his wounds, but there was an even greater surprise. In a far corner, in the light of the flickering fire, were heaps of coins and bars of gold. 'Is that Flint's treasure?' I asked, hardly able to tear my eyes from the shining pile of wealth.

'That's *some* of it,' Captain Smollett replied. 'And we have paid a heavy price for that much.'

It was true. This was only a part of Flint's treasure. We had come so far to find it, and yet it had already cost the lives of seventeen men from the *Hispaniola*. I found myself wondering if it was worth it.

Chapter Seventeen

Ben Gunn's cave was well-stocked with goat meat. We sat and ate while the doctor and Ben told me what had happened while I had gone back to free the *Hispaniola*.

'During the many years I spent marooned here, I found some of Flint's treasure, dug it up and, piece by piece, brought it back to this cave,' Ben explained.

'When I discovered this,' the doctor said, 'I thought it best to let Silver have the treasure map, along with the hut and all the supplies. They could go on a wild treasure hunt while we escaped the island.'

The next morning, we had the difficult job of carrying all the treasure down to the *Hispaniola*. It was a big job for so few of us and it took three days. Since I was not as strong as the others, I was given the job of sorting the coins into money bags. It was a strange collection, with coins from many parts of the world. My back ached from having to sit bent over the coins, and my fingers were sore from sorting them.

We hadn't heard anything from the escaped pirates. But on the third day, the doctor and I heard shrieking and singing, and knew they were near. We discussed what we should do. The pirates were too dangerous to take back with us on the *Hispaniola*. We decided to leave them on the island and left some supplies for them: salted goat, medicine, tools, clothes, weapons, rope and a spare sail.

When we had made sure that we had enough water and supplies on the *Hispaniola* for our journey home, we pulled up the repaired anchor and were ready to leave. The pirates must have been watching us more closely than we thought, because they fired at us from the shore. I kept undercover as the ship pulled away from the island. When I next dared to look out, I was overjoyed to see Treasure Island disappearing into the distance.

We were so short of men that everyone on board had to help sail the ship. Only the injured captain lay on a mattress, giving his orders. We sailed for the nearest port in Central America – we could not risk the long voyage home without rest and some more crew.

We reached Central America at dusk. I was very happy to see so many friendly faces, taste delicious tropical fruit and see lights shining in the town, after our dark and terrifying adventure on Treasure Island. I went ashore with the

doctor and the squire and we met a friendly sea captain, who invited us and all the crew to dinner on board his ship. We were all eager to go, even the injured Captain Smollett, but Silver refused. Ben decided to remain too. 'Someone has to guard the ship,' he said with a look at Silver. We had such a great time that we didn't return to the *Hispaniola* until the morning.

We found Ben Gunn on the deck alone. 'Silver has stolen a bag of coins and fled,' he told us.

In truth, we were glad to be rid of him.

With a few more sailors on board, we finally set sail and had a good journey home to England.

Of all the men who had sailed to Treasure Island on the *Hispaniola*, only five returned: myself, Doctor Livesey, Squire Trelawney, Captain Smollett and Abraham Gray. Although we were allowed to keep some of the treasure, much of it remains on the island where Flint buried it. I'm happy to leave it there –

I never want to go back to that place again.

Nothing was ever heard of Silver again. But I still have bad dreams in which I hear the voice of the parrot, Captain Flint, ringing in my ears and squawking: 'Pieces of eight! Pieces of eight! Pieces of eight!'

Robert Louis Stevenson

Robert Louis Stevenson was born in Edinburgh in 1850. Despite very poor health, he wrote many books and travelled widely. His travels inspired him to write one of his most famous tales, *Treasure Island*. The story was published in separate parts between 1881 and 1882 in a children's magazine called *Young Folks*, before being published as a book in 1883. Today Stevenson is one of the most translated authors in the world.